MGM's
TOM and JERRY'S
MERRY CHRISTMAS

TOLD BY PETER ARCHER

PICTURES BY M-G-M CARTOONS
ADAPTED BY
HARVEY EISENBERG AND SAMUEL ARMSTRONG

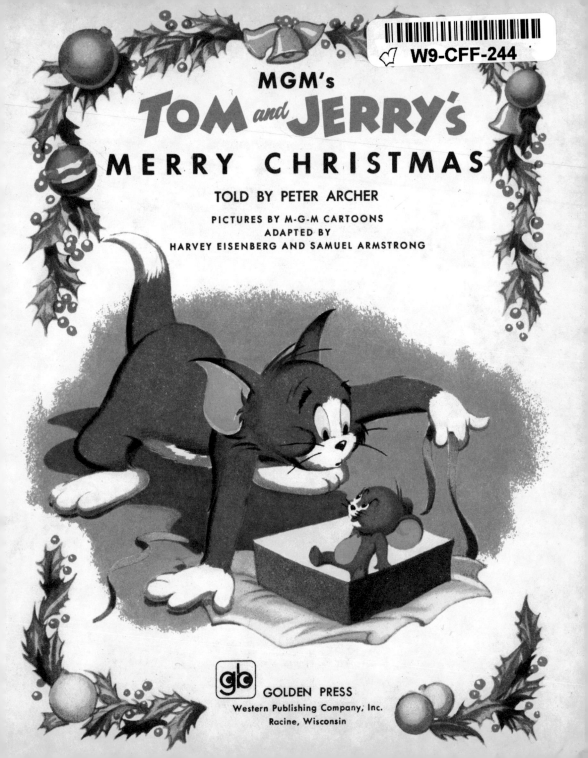

GOLDEN PRESS
Western Publishing Company, Inc.
Racine, Wisconsin

Ninth Printing, 1973

GOLDEN, A LITTLE GOLDEN BOOK®, and GOLDEN PRESS®
are trademarks of Western Publishing Company, Inc.

JERRY MOUSE hung up his Christmas stocking, and a stocking for his little friend Tuffy.

Then he went to the door of the mousehole and peeped out.

Tom Cat was crouched in the Big Peoples' kitchen, not two squares away from the mousehole. And he was watching it closely.

"We'll never get so much as a crumb to put in our stockings unless he goes away," said Jerry.

And that Tom certainly didn't mean to do.

He meant to guard all the goodies in the kitchen and on the tree, so that Cook would give him a fine, big helping of Christmas dinner.

"Cheer up," said Jerry. "There's a way to get rid of him!" And he ran into the living room, and started to saw a new mousehole door.

"What's that noise?" cried Tom, tiptoeing out of the kitchen and along the wall to the place where Jerry was working.

"Now you saw," Jerry whispered to Tuffy.

The minute Tuffy began, Jerry Mouse scurried out the back door with a pillowcase over his shoulder.

He was soon filling it with candy and nuts and stuffed dates. But as he backed past the heaping bowls, he bumped into one filled with cranberry sauce which was too near the edge.

Crash-splash! Down to the floor it went!

"What was that?" Tom cried. He came racing into the kitchen just in time to see Jerry, bag and all, disappear into the mousehole.

Then Tom saw the cranberry sauce.

"If Cook sees that," he moaned, "there'll be no Christmas Dinner for me!"

And little as he liked it, lick, lick, lick—he began to lick up every last bit.

While Tom was busy at that, Jerry and Tuffy finished their new door, and peeped out at the Big Peoples' Christmas tree.

It was so beautiful that they both gasped.

"Oh!" sighed Tuffy. "I'd like to have that little horn that's way up near the top!"

And Jerry squeaked, "I'd like to have that little drum!" Then both those mice must have had the same idea at the same time—

—because they both smiled secret smiles. And when Jerry seemed to be sound asleep, Tuffy went tiptoeing out the back door.

He soon came back with the little drum, hid it under his bed, and hopped in himself.

He squeezed his eyes shut and snored away as if he'd been there all the time.

"Asleep at last!" said Jerry, stealing out the front door and up the Big Peoples' tree.

"Tuffy will have a merry Christmas, anyway," he
thought, as he unhooked the little horn.

But just as Jerry got to the bottom of the tree,

whom did he see creeping between him and the mousehole—but his enemy Tom Cat!

Poor Jerry! He flattened himself against the trunk, sure that he was done for this time!

And then he saw that Tom wasn't even trying to catch him!

Instead, that old cat was carrying a beautiful mouse-sized tree, all trimmed with bits of popcorn and tasty cheese, and tiny candy beads.

While Jerry watched, he pushed it through their new door and backed away, looking just about as sheepish as a cat ever looked, and murmuring, "Oh well, Christmas comes but once a year—"

"What do you know about that!" gasped Jerry.

He put Tuffy's present under that beautiful little
tree, and hurried into the bedroom.

"Wake up, Tuffy," he said. "Come with me!"

Then Jerry led Tuffy to their store room, because it took them both to get out the big, brand-new can of sardines that he had hidden there.

Tied with red ribbon, and propped against Tom's bowl, it made a most wonderful present!

"But why give *him* a present?" asked Tuffy.

Instead of answering, Jerry took him in to see their Christmas tree.

"It's from Tom Cat. Tom Cat gave it to us!" he said. "And the horn is from me." Soon the two little mice were merrily playing carols.

It wasn't long until Tom found his present, too.
"For me!" he cried. "They got a present for me!"
With happy tears in his eyes, he began to purr the
same tune that Jerry and Tuffy were playing.

—and down they sat, one on each side of Tom Cat, while all three, grinning from ear to ear, played and sang in close harmony:

"A very merry Christmas to ALL!"